THERE'S A MONSTER UNDER MY BED

James Howe

Illustrated by
David Rose

Aladdin Books
Macmillan Publishing Company
New York

First Aladdin Books edition 1990

Aladdin Books
Macmillan Publishing Company
866 Third Avenue, New York, NY 10022
Collier Macmillan Canada, Inc.

Printed in the United States of America

A hardcover edition of There's a Monster under My Bed
is available from Atheneum, Macmillan Publishing Company.

10 9 8 7 6 5 4 3 2

Library of Congress Cataloging-in-Publication Data
Howe, James, 1946–
There's a monster under my bed / James Howe,
illustrated by David Rose.
    p. cm.
   Reprinted. Originally published: New York:
Atheneum, 1986.
   Summary: Simon is sure there are monsters under
his bed in the night—he can even hear them breathing.
   ISBN 0–689–71409–2
   [1.Night—Fiction.   2. Fear—Fiction.   3. Monsters—Fiction.]
I. Rose, David S., 1947– ill. II. Title.
PZ7.H83727Th 1990
[E]—dc20 89–18664 CIP AC

This edition is reprinted by arrangement with Atheneum
Publishers, an imprint of Macmillan Publishing Company.

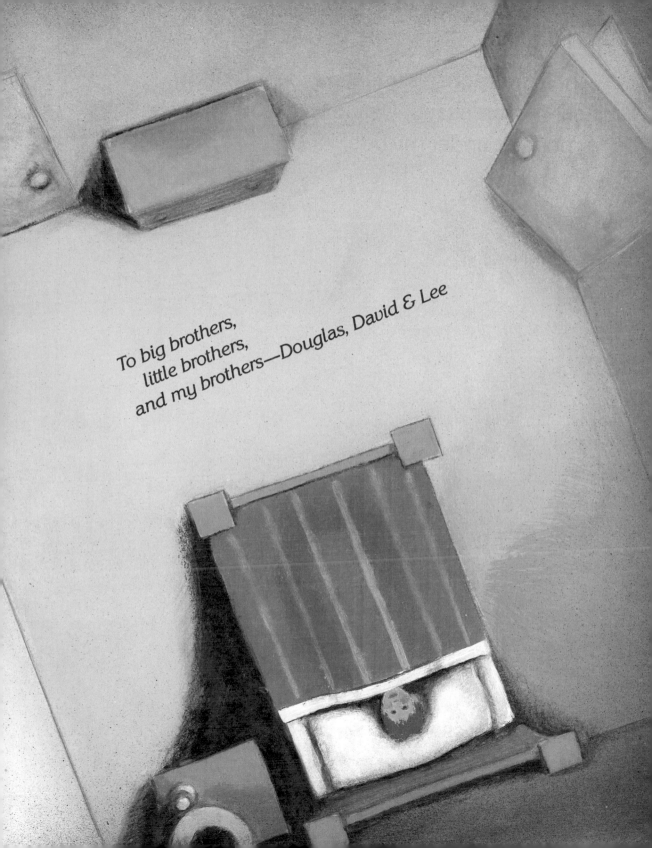

To big brothers,
  little brothers,
  and my brothers—Douglas, David & Lee

There's a monster under my bed. I can hear him breathing. Listen. I told you. There's a monster under my bed.

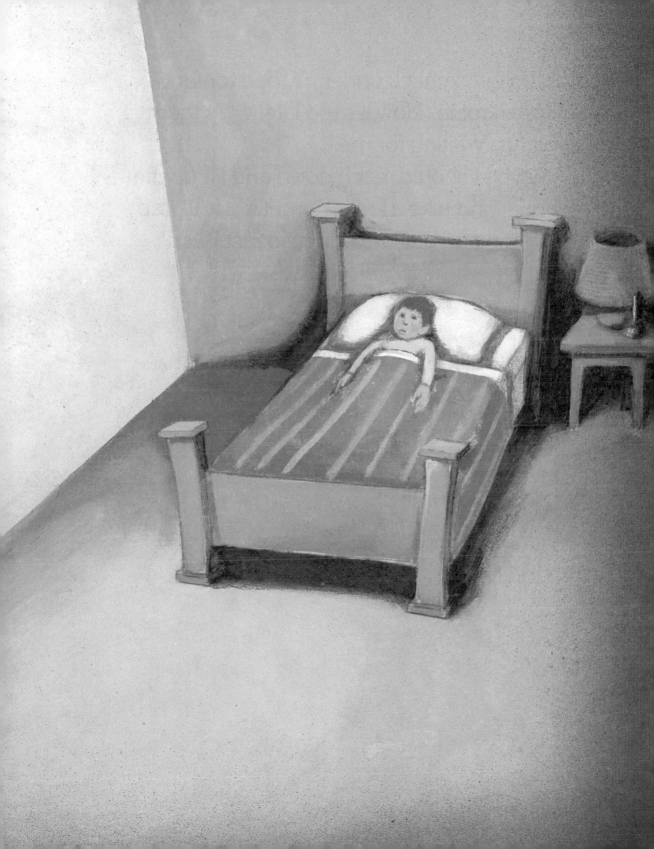

I forgot to check under my bed tonight before I got in. Now it's too late. *He*'s there. Waiting. Waiting for me.

Maybe I should reach down and lift up the blanket and take a look. Forget it. He'll grab my hand and pull me under so fast I won't even have time to yell for Dad.

What if my foot slips over the edge while I'm asleep? He'll bite it off, that's what.

I think I'll lie in the middle of the bed. And not move. And stay awake. All night.

Why did I have to tell Mom I was too old for a night light? I can't see anything in here. Alex has a night light. But he's a baby. Not like me.

Did you feel that? The mattress jumped.
I *felt* it. Right there, under my leg. It went
"Pop!" There *is* a monster under my bed.

Or maybe there are two. Two hairy monsters playing hide-and-go-seek. No, monsters don't play games. They're fighting. Fighting over who gets to eat me.

Maybe there are three. Three slimy monsters sharpening their claws. Hear them? I'd better run. No, they'll grab me before I can get to the door.

There could be four. Four fat monsters
making a fire to fry me up.
It's getting hot in here.

There might be five. Five drooly monsters crawling up the sides of my bed. I'll scream. Uh-uh, that's what Alex would do.

What if there are more? More and more
monsters coming to get me.

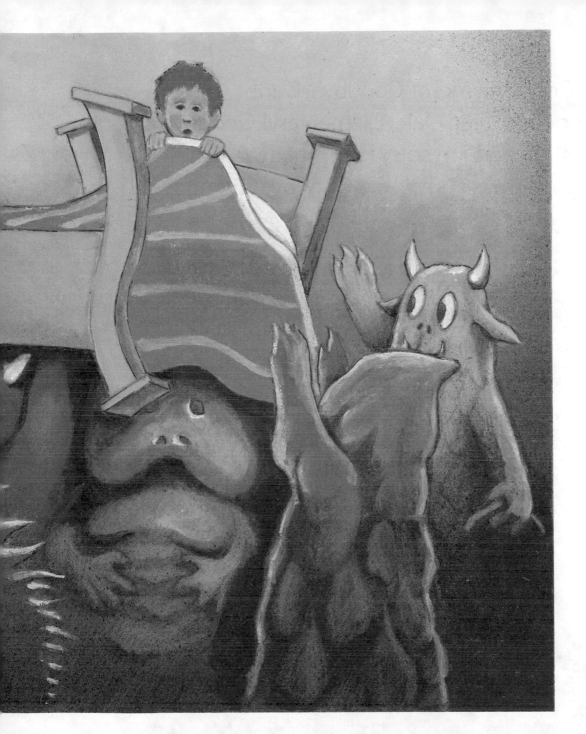

Coming to munch me for a midnight
snack!

Goodbye, Mom! Goodbye, Dad!
Goodbye, Glen Oaks Elementary! Goodbye,
Mrs. Grover! I'm sorry I put that dead fish
in your drawer last week. Goodbye, Grandpa!
Goodbye —

What's this? The flashlight Mom left. "Just in case," she said. In case of what? In case of *monsters,* of course.

I know. I'll jump down and shine the light in the monsters' eyes. That'll scare them away. Ready? One...two...three.

Look! See his eyes? Hear his breathing? I'm going to faint. There *is* a monster under my bed!

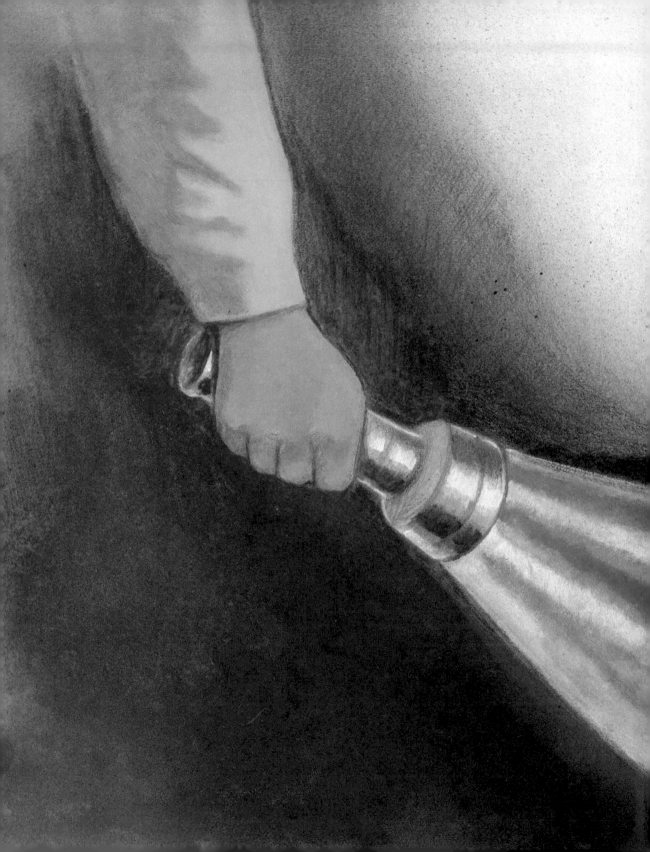

"Alex!"

"Hi, Simon."

"What are you doing there?"

"Hiding. There's a monster under my bed."

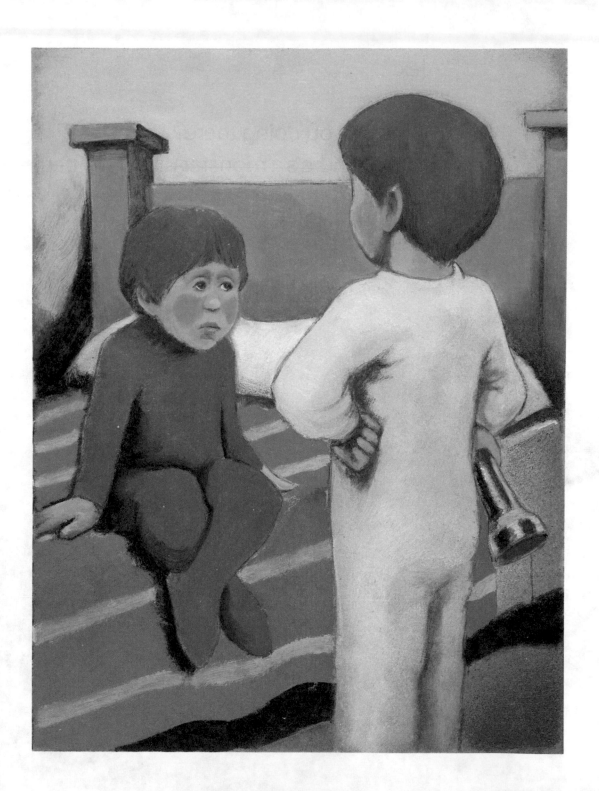

"What are you doing with that flashlight?"

"Me? Oh, nothing. I was just looking for something."

"Monsters?"

"Of course not. There's no such things as monsters. Don't be a baby."

"There *was* a monster under my bed, Simon. Want to see?"

"Uh. . . no thanks. I have a better idea."

"What?"

"Why don't you sleep in here with me tonight? That way you won't be scared."

"Good night, Alex."

"Good night, Simon. Simon?"

"What?"

"I feel safe in here. You know why, Simon. You know why?"

"Why?"

"Because you won't let the monsters get me. Will you, Simon?"

"Of course not, Alex. After all, what's a brother for?"